W9-BYR-110

CHOOSE YOUR OWN TRACK

MYSTERY OF THE
TRANSCONTINENTAL RAILROAD

Roberta Baxter

Copyright © 2019 Roberta Baxter
All rights reserved.
ISBN: 9781077453364

BEFORE YOU READ THIS BOOK!

You will have to make choices as you read this book. You will see *Choose Your Own Track* at the end of sections. You must choose where to go next. At any time, you can go back and make a different choice and see where the adventure takes you. You are in charge of the track you choose.
ALL ABOARD!

"But, Mom, I don't want to go to Mr. Chaney's house. He's way too creepy. You take the stuff to him,"

"Dylan O'Neill, I want you to go and…" Before Mom could say more, your little brother and cousin bounce down the stairs.

"We're building a Lego City around our train tracks, Dylan. Want to come?" your brother, Christopher, says.

"First, I want all three of you boys to deliver this soup and brownies to Mr. Chaney," Mom says. "He had surgery on his shoulder and he needs some help." Looking at you, she says, "You might find out that he's an interesting man. He has a big collection of something that you really like. Maybe you can see it."

What could that spooky old man collect that you like: Legos, trains, rocks, dinosaur books. But before you can think, you, Christopher and David are out the door with the food. You trudge across the street and Christopher knocks on the door of Mr. Chaney's house.

After a few minutes, the door opens slowly and you see Mr. Chaney's wiry, wild hair and wrinkled face looking at you.

David speaks up and says, "We brought you some food from Aunt Lynn. Can we see your collection?"

Mr. Chaney glares another minute and then pulls open the door. As you step inside, you see that his right arm is in a sling that wraps around his waist. He looks really uncomfortable.

"You want to see my collection, huh," he says in a rough, deep voice. He looks at the three of you and continues, "Do I know you?"

You finally find your voice and say, "I'm Dylan and this is my brother, Christopher, and my cousin, David. We live across the street."

He stares at you a while longer and then says, "Thank your mother for the food. She is kind. You can put it in the kitchen. Do all of you live over there?"

"I don't live there," David says. "I'm just visiting for Spring

1

Break."

When Christopher comes back from the kitchen, Mr. Chaney points to a door. "My collection is down there, but if you see it, you can't tell other boys. I don't want the whole city coming in here to bother me."

Choose Your Track: Do you go downstairs to the basement? Go to page 8

Choose Your Track: Do you go home and stay away from Mr. Chaney? Go to page 48

When the magic watch stops your travel, you are behind a bush near the flat place far ahead of the train. You hear *whang, whang* as the trackbuilders pound spikes into the rails.

The whole area is full of men. Some are carrying rails from nearby wagons. Others are swinging hammers. You see a boy about your age carrying boxes. He sees you and comes closer.

"My name is Ryan," he says. "Are you looking for a job here?"

"We would like to see how the track is built," Christopher says.

You follow Ryan as he carries a box of spikes toward the front edge of the tracks. Ahead you see a smooth dirt path packed down like a road. It stretches into the distance. Men are pulling railroad ties, heavy pieces of wood, out of wagons. They plunk the ties down across the graded dirt.

Behind the men placing ties, wagons full of metal rails pull forward. The drivers jockey the horses to get as close to the ties as possible. Five men grab each rail and hoist it out of the wagon. They lug it forward. A man yells "Down" and they drop the rail onto the ties. At the same time, five more men are placing the opposite rail. The men go back for another rail. A man with a bar jumps forward and measures the distance between the two rails just laid down. Men with hammers finish the last rail and move forward to pound spikes into the new rails.

Ryan says, "You can help me with the spikes if you want."

Before you start to the wagon where the spikes are, David asks, "What are they doing with the stick the man puts between the rails?"

"That man is a gauger," Ryan says. "The gauge is the measurement between the rails. If it is not right, the trains won't run or they might even derail. It has to be exact, so they measure it on each rail."

As you begin to haul boxes of spikes forward to where the rails are going down, you ask, "How heavy are those rails that it takes five men to lift them?"

Ryan says, "I was told that they weigh 500 pounds each. King Kelly has the nickname of "King" because they had a contest one Saturday and he lifted more than anyone else in camp. But even he can't lift one rail by himself."

David was watching the spikers. He said, "They pound each spike three times. They must be strong to do that."

"They are the best," Ryan says. "Three strokes to a spike, 10 spikes to a rail, four hundred rails to a mile. And they do it day after day. Usually we can lay about 2 miles of track a day."

"That's 12,000 strokes in a mile," you say.

Ryan looks at you with surprise. "That was fast," he says.

You shrug. "I'm good at math."

You finish unloading the boxes of spikes from that wagon. Ryan is going with the driver to get more spikes.

You say, "We will watch a little longer."

After the wagon rattles off and another takes its place, you motion for Christopher and David to follow you behind a bush next to the tracks.

"I want to see what the men at the very front are doing," you say.

"Should we waste time?" Christopher asks. "How much time do we have left?"

You pull the watch out of your pocket. It shows 5 hours left.

"We'll have time if we use it to travel," you say. "That will go faster."

"Okay," Christopher says, "but it will have to be quick."

4

You point the hand on the second crystal to the 9 and push down. Once the dark squeezing stops, you see that you are far ahead of the rest of the train builders. You can barely see a puff of smoke from the locomotives in the distance behind you. In front of you, men are shoveling dirt as others are driving horses pulling a low box behind them, flattening the ground.

A little further ahead, men are pounding pick axes into the ground and using them to pry up large rocks. So this is where the transcontinental track building starts.

"Let's go," David says, pulling on your arm.

You go behind a wagon, but before you can pull the watch out of your pocket, your arms are grabbed from behind. You try to yell, but your voice is stuck in your throat. Then your heart drops as you see that Christopher and David are pulling and kicking to get away from two men that have them by the arms. The men are painted with bright colors and have feathers sticking out of their heads. You remember that in the days of the transcontinental railroad, these natives were called Indians. They did not want people on their land. *What have I gotten Christopher and David into?*

The men wrap cloths around your mouths so you can't yell and they throw you up on to horses. They jump up behind you and slowly ride the horses away from the track. Once they are sure that no one is coming after them, they kick the horses into a gallop.

You hang on to the horse's mane as best you can, but you would probably fall if the man wasn't holding you. You can see from the corner of your eye that Christopher and David are barely hanging on, too.

In what seems like a long time, you arrive at a village. People come around to point at you and laugh. Some of them are boys that look like your age. They make faces and pretend to throw rocks at you.

Finally, the men pull you off of the horses. They tie your hands behind your back with leather straps and then tie you to Christopher and David. They push onto the floor of one of their teepees and leave the three of you alone.

"Dylan, this is scary," David says.

"I know, but I'm thinking," you say with a shake in your voice.

Your brain seems to be moving slowly and thoughts just slip away. Then you think of the watch.

"I've got an idea," you say. "Let's see if we can get to the watch. Christopher, can you reach as far as my pocket and pull it out?

Christopher begins to twist and pull against the straps. You and David scoot close to each other's backs to give Christopher some slack.

Christopher's fingers reach your pocket, but it is a long time before he can undo the button. Using two fingers, he stretches and reaches into the pocket. He manages to clamp the watch with his fingers and pull it out. Then, whoops, it drops onto the floor.

"I think I can grab it," David says. You scrunch around again to give him room and he uses a finger to scoot the watch over. Finally, he pulls it into his hand.

You realize that you have been holding your breath. You breathe again and say, "Do you think you can hold it, David and one of us can push the crystal?"

"I think so," David agrees.

"Where should we go?" you ask. "Should we try to get back to the railroad or go all the way home?"

"We should use the stem to go home," Christopher says. "But we have to hurry before those men come back."

"Maybe we can get back to the railroad," you say. Outside you can hear people talking and laughing and someone is talking loud, like making a speech. "We can't do rock, paper, scissors with our hands tied, but let's decide what we are going to try to do."

Choose Your Track: Do you choose to go to the railroad site? Go to page 27.

Choose Your Track: Do you choose to go home? Go to page 19.

You nod and start to say something, but Christopher and David are already heading to the door. You follow and Mr. Chaney shuffles along behind.

You head down the stairs, but below is only darkness until one of the boys finds a light switch. Then you see that Christopher stops abruptly at the bottom of the stairs and David bumps into him.

From the fourth stair up, you see why they stopped. Taking up most of the basement is a gigantic train table. Not just any train table. Huge mountains at one end flow into low flat areas at the other. You see a few tunnels through the mountains and bridges across deep canyons. On the tracks are two locomotives, made like old steam engines, with train cars stretched out behind them.

Mr. Chaney says, "Go on down, boys, and we'll turn it on."

You step down the last of the stairs with your eyes fixed on those magnificent trains. Then you notice that Christopher and David are not looking at the train table. They are pointing at the walls of the basement. Your eyes open even wider when you see that every inch of the walls is covered with shelves holding more trains—some very modern looking, some steam engines. This is really some collection.

You turn to ask Mr. Chaney where he got all of these trains, but before you say anything, he reaches for a switch on the train table and the trains start up. To your amazement, the locomotives are puffing out white smoke. One train behind the other, they move quickly across the flat section and slow down as they chug up the mountains and through the tunnels.

You look at Mr. Chaney again and he answers before you can ask. "This is a model of the transcontinental railroad. Have you heard of it?"

"I've heard of it, but I don't know much," you answer. You sit on the floor, level with the table, watching as the trains circle. Both of the big engines are pulling a coal car and then a bunch of other cars.

"In the 1850s, people started planning to build a railroad all the way across the United States. Then you could only travel from the East Coast to California by traveling in a ship around South America or by ..."

"Wagon train," Christopher says. "I learned that in school."

"Right," Mr. Chaney agreed. "And either way took a long time, several months. A train would be much faster. So they started plans to build the transcontinental railroad. Transcontinental just means it goes across the entire continent."

"When did they build it?" David asked.

Before Mr. Chaney could answer, they heard a ding-dong above the sound of the trains rolling around the track.

Choose Your Track: Go to page 17.

You start to trudge along the track. The dining car seems far away and the sun is hot. You can see mostly flat land with no houses or towns are in sight.

Then David tugs on your sleeve. "Hey, Dylan," he says. "We should use that watch. It will get us there faster."

You gulp as you realize that you haven't looked at that magic watch since you got here. *What if you are running out of time!*

You unbutton your pocket and pull out the watch. Christopher and David crowd around as you raise the top crystal. "Whew," you say. "We still have 5 hours."

Just then some men jostle you as they walk along the track. "We better get out of sight before we travel with the watch," you say.

But which way to go, you think as you pull out the watch. Before you can ask, David says, "We need to go a little bit west."

The younger boys look down at the watch while you point the hand at the 9. You push down on the crystal and again you feel that dark, squeezing feeling. When you open your eyes, you are a few yards away from the track and next to the engineer's car when you met Mack Brown. The dining car is a few more cars ahead. The train is creeping forward, so the three of you jog along and jump up on the step into the car.

The dining car is full of long tables. Dozens of plates are already on the tables. David reaches over and tries to pick one up. It is nailed to the table.

"How do they wash them?" David wonders.

Before you can figure that out, the train stops and the whistle blows. Men swarm from the front of the train to the dining car. A man comes out of the kitchen and says, "Hey, you boys! Get to work."

Next thing you know, you have a big pot of stew to carry as the men fill up their plates from it. You can barely fit through the rows of

10

tables full of men.

You see Christopher with a bucket of coffee. He is squeezing between the tables and David is not far behind him with another bucket. Suddenly, a huge man jumps up from the table. His arm hits the bucket that Christopher is holding and coffee splashes out on the man's leg.

"You boy!" the man yells. He grabs Christopher by the neck and almost lifts him off the floor. Without thinking, you jump across the table in front of you and try to pull Christopher out of the man's hands. David is next to you trying to help.

You kick at the man's leg and he lets Christopher go.

Then he turns to you. "What do you think, kicking me like that!"

"That's my brother and no one hurts my brother." Christopher is gasping as he struggles to catch his breath.

"And who is this pipsqueak?" the man asks as David squeezes in next to you.

"I'm their cousin," David says.

"Well, the whole family is ready to take on King Kelly," the man says and then he laughs. "Who might you be?"

"Dylan O'Neill," you answer.

"Oh, and a good Irish name it is," the man says. "Go along then and protect your family, but watch out with that coffee."

The three of you head back to the kitchen as a big group of men are leaving. They step across from table to table until they reach the door. *What would Mom think of that—walking on the table?*

The cook hands you a small mop and bucket full of water and says, "Get to work on those plates."

"What?" you ask.

"Just swab them out before the next group gets here to eat." He turns and goes back into the kitchen car.

When you look at Christopher and David, you see a look of horror on their faces. You probably have the same look.

"That's gross! Let's get out of here," David says.

"Yeah, germs and more germs," Christopher agrees. "Let's go see if we can find any clues on the thieves. So far, all we've done is work."

You sneak over to a plate full of bread and grab three pieces. "Maybe this will keep us going for a while without eating that germy food," you say.

Choose Your Own Track: do you choose to go to see the locomotives? Go to page 24.

Choose Your Own Track: do you choose to go see the track builders? Go to page 3.

You look at Christopher and David and they nod. Your heart is pounding, but you say, "Yes," as you move closer to your brother and your cousin.

Mr. Chaney flips the switch to stop the trains. He grabs the smokestack of Engine 109. "This is the engine for the Union Pacific Railroad. It will send you back in time. Use the pocket watch to come back home. Don't use up all the time. Good travels."

He twists the engine's smokestack. You feel like your body is being squeezed and it seems like the air in your lungs is gone. Everything goes black and you start to panic. Then suddenly, you can see and breathe again. You can hear Christopher and David pulling in breaths next to you. You feel hot air on your face as you open your eyes.

Ahead of you is a small hill and you can hear cows mooing. *What is this?* You thought you would see a railroad. The three of you creep up the hill and look over. You see thousands of cows in front of you. *What in the world? Did you go to the wrong time or the wrong place? Should you go back to Mr. Chaney?*

As the three of you are discussing it, you hear a train whistle. *Maybe this is not the wrong place.* You look over the hill again and see that a train stretches up a hill way ahead of the cattle. Wagons pulled by mules and oxen are following the train.

"Let's go," you say, even though your mind is not sure about this action.

You circle around the cattle and climb up a small hill. The sun is shining as you push through some scrubby bushes. You can feel the sweat breaking out on your forehead. Once you get to the top and look over, you see a train and a lot of men. The land around the tracks is mostly flat with a few hills and green bushes.

"Looks like the right place," Christopher says.

"That train is backward," David says.

You can see that David is right. Three locomotives are pushing the train cars forward, instead of pulling them. The three of you jog along the track until you catch up with the locomotives. They are chugging forward slowly and then they stop. You can feel the power of their engines as the sound pumps through your body. The locomotives have "Union Pacific" written in big letters on the sides. When you look up, you can see the engineer with his hand on the throttle. You wish you could climb up there with him.

But you need to find Mack Brown, so you pass the locomotives and continue on to the train cars.

Some of the cars are boxcars. Far ahead you can see flatcars. One has men working on top and you can see smoke coming up from what they are doing. You catch a smell of food as you walk forward.

David spots a small sign on one of the boxcars that says "Engineer's Office." Maybe you can find Mack Brown there. You look at the other two boys and they nod, so you knock on the door, just as the train starts slowly forward again.

The door opens. You boys jog along with the train and you ask the man in the door if he knows where Mack Brown is.

"You found him," the man says. "Are you here from Tom Chaney?"

"Yes," you answer.

"Come aboard."

You jump onto the step and reach back to help Christopher. Just then the train stops again, so he and David climb up.

The walls inside the boxcar are covered with maps. The table has papers everywhere and on one you can see a drawing for a bridge.

Before you can think of what to say to Mr. Brown, David blurts out, "Why is the train backwards?
Mr. Brown smiles and says, "Good question. We put the

supplies that the tracklayers need at the front of the train—the rails, ties, spikes. We have a blacksmith shop and a carpenter shop to fix things that break. Then we have a sleeping car, a kitchen, and a dining hall. All this needs to be at the front, so the men can get to the supplies. So we put the locomotives at the back to push."

He pointed toward the back of the train. "The cattle are for food and all those wagons are carrying supplies, some of it from as far away as Omaha."

"Mr. Chaney told us there is a big problem, a thief or something," you say.

"Yes, a lot of stealing has been going on. We've lost lots of supplies and that costs money," Mr. Brown says. "We haven't figured out how it's happening, so I thought we could use some help from Tom. I didn't know he was sending boys this time."

"He had surgery on his shoulder, so he can't use that arm," you explain. "So he sent us."

Christopher asks, "What supplies are being stolen?"

"Every kind of thing that we need," Mr. Brown says. "Spikes, food items, hammers. I'm not sure what you boys can do, but maybe if you keep your eyes and ears open, you might hear something that would help catch the thieves. If you find out something, come and find me. Don't try to catch the criminals on your own. Now, would you like to see this perpetual train?"

"Why do they call it that?" Christopher asks.

"It's always moving to keep up with the track builders."

You feel the train start to again as Mr. Brown opens the door. He steps down to the ground easily and you and the others jump out. The train stops again and you walk to the front. Mr. Brown points out the blacksmith shop, the dining car, the sleeping car and the kitchens. Then someone comes up and says, "Mack, we need you up at the end of track."

15

"Good luck, boys," Mr. Brown says as he walks away.

Before you can decide what to do next, a man walks by with a big wagon wheel. "Out of the way, boys," he yells.

"Where should we go first?" David asks.

"I'm not sure," you say. "Should we go up front to see the track builders?"

"Maybe we should check out the wagons," Christopher says. "They carry the supplies."

"Let's go see the locomotives," David says.

You want to see the locomotives and the track builders. How can you decide what to do? Then you have an idea.

"I say the track builders first, then the locomotives if the engineers will let us, and then the wagons," you say.

"The supplies are coming in by wagon," Christopher says. "If we check them out first, we'll have time to see the track builders and locomotives later."

"Rock, paper, scissors," you say. "That way we can all three decide.

All three of you pound your fist on your hand. "One, two, three," you say. Christopher comes up with rock, but you and David show paper.

You pull out the watch so you can travel faster. You point the hand on the second crystal and then push down.

Choose Your Track: If you choose to go to track builders, go to page 3.

Choose Your Track: If you choose to check out the wagons first, go to page 34.

"Excuse me, boys. That's my telegraph. I need to see what the message is." Mr. Chaney goes to a flat part of the train table and pulls a strip of paper out of a slot at the bottom.

"The message comes from the telegraph office on the table," he says, pointing to a small building next to the tracks where they passed through a small town.

He begins to read the strip of paper. You can see that it is not covered with letters, but with dots and lines. Mr. Chaney pulls a stub of a pencil out of his pocket and starts writing on the paper below the shapes. He can only use one hand because of the sling, so the paper is scooting around. Christopher reaches out and holds the paper still so Mr. Chaney can keep writing.

"What is that kind of writing?" David asks.

"It's Morse code," Mr. Chaney says. "Have you heard of that?"

"I have," you remember. "I only know dot, dot, dot, dash, dash, dash, dot, dot, dot means SOS, get help."

"That's right. Every letter and number has a combination of dots and dashes and you can decipher the message by following the code."

Mr. Chaney was silent for a while after he finished the message. Then he says, "There is trouble in Nebraska with the construction of the transcontinental railroad. They need help to catch a thief, but I can't go with this sling. I'm useless to them."

Your mind is confused. *How can he receive messages from the transcontinental railroad builders? That was a long time ago. How can he help them? That railroad is already finished, right?*

Before you can figure things out, Mr. Chaney looks at you and says, "How old are you?"

Without thinking, you answer, "I'm 11."

"That's pretty young, but I think you can do it."

"Do what?"

"You can go to the building site of the transcontinental railroad and help them find a thief who is slowing everything down."

"Me…?" you start to talk, but Christopher interrupts. "We'll go, too. All three of us can help. I'm eight, he's seven, we're big enough."

"But, how…." you say.

"Here's how it works," Mr. Chaney says. He reaches into a box near the track and pulls something out. He places it in your hand and you see that it is an old-fashioned pocket watch. "This looks like any pocket watch, but it is special. Magic, actually," he says. "Don't do anything with it yet."

Choose Your Track: Go to page 30.

You choose to go home. Someone else can solve the mystery of the thief on the transcontinental railroad.

THE END

When the squeezing stops, you open your eyes and realize that it is cold. You are standing on a snowy ledge with a huge mountain behind you. You can hear a few voices and then suddenly there is a loud bang!

"What was that?" Christopher asks.

"I'm not sure," you say. "Let's go look."

You walk carefully along the ledge to peek around a big rock. Ahead of you is a tunnel. A cloud of smoke and dust is flying out of the tunnel and a few men are slowly walking inside. A locomotive and a couple of train cars are standing just outside the tunnel. The cars are loaded with ties and rails and other supplies, just like the train in Nebraska. But this locomotive says "Central Pacific" on the side and it is in front of the train, not the back.

"They must have just set off some explosive," you say. "We should stay away from there, but where do we go?"

David suddenly waves his hand and a teenage boy from down near the tunnel waves back. "Let's go talk to him," David says.

When you get to the boy, you can see that he is Chinese. He is wearing a blanket wrapped around a blue shirt and he has a pointed bowl hat.

"You look for work?" the boy asks.

"We wanted to see the railroad being built," you say.

"You need food. We have food," he says.

Before you can say anything else, he turns and walks into a hole in the snowbank. You look at Christopher and David and then you all follow him.

Once you are through the hole, you can see that a tunnel dug in deep snow stretch out ahead of you. You can see other tunnels branching off.

"Wow," David says. "It's like the biggest snow cave ever."

You follow the boy and he leads you into a space where a small fire is burning. A pot has something cooking in it. Some men are sitting around the fire. When you look up, you can see that you are inside a tent, but it is surrounded by snow.

Christopher asks, "How did you get these tents under the snow?"

The boy says, "The tents here, the snow come."

"My name is Dylan," you tell the boy. "This is Christopher and David."

"My name Fang," the boys says. "You work railroad?"

"Uh, our father does," you say. "We want to see the builders. Do you know a man named Dan Carson? He's supposed to show us around."

"Dan Carson is on other side of tunnel," Fang says. So you won't have any help from Mr. Carson.

Just then the men sitting around the fire stand up and start down a snow tunnel. Fang goes, too, so you follow him. After a short walk, you see the end of the big tunnel ahead.

"Where are we going, Fang?" you ask.

"We help men get tools to start dig," he says.

Just inside the mouth of the tunnel are several wheelbarrows full of tools, like pick axes and hammers. As the men walk by, Fang hands them what they ask for. You start to hand Fang the tools when he tells you in English what the man said in Chinese.

You get a pretty good rhythm going and then suddenly, one of the men yells. The head of the pick ax that you handed Fang fell off and almost hit the man's foot. The man is talking in fast Chinese and you wonder if he will come after you.

"I didn't make it do that," you tell Fang.

He waves you to be quiet, as the man examines the head and handle of the pick ax. The other men gather around. The man begins to show the pieces to the other men and they discuss what they see in Chinese.

"What's going on?" David asks.

Fang says, "The men say that the ax head was hurt, damaged…"

"You mean sabotage?" you ask.

"I not know that word," Fang says.

Christopher chimes in. "It means someone did it deliberately to slow down the work."

"Yes, that is good word," Fang says. "We have had many things like this. The men are worried."

The men gather up the rest of the tools and head into the tunnel. You can see that the hole reaches in a way and then stops at a rock wall. In front of the wall are piles of rocks that must have been blasted loose in the explosion you heard.

"They will work," Fang says. "We go make tea."

As you walk back to the buried tents, you ask Fang, "What else has happened?"

"One day, all fuses gone," he says. "Can't blast until find fuses or more come? Took long time to get more from California. Another time, man pulling rocks up from hole in middle of tunnel and rope breaks. No one hurt, but worried."

You follow Fang into the snow tents to a place where a large kettle of water is steaming on a fire. Fang throws something into the water and you see that it must be tea. Then he sits down to wait until the tea is ready.

22

Nearby are buckets hooked to a stick, two buckets on each stick. You're not sure what they are for until Fang starts to dip the tea into the buckets and lifts the stick up to his shoulders.

"We carry to men so they can drink," he tells you.

You pick up a bucket set and so does Christopher. There aren't any more buckets, so David will not have a load.

Fang reaches over with a dipper of tea and starts to fill up one of your buckets. When it is full, he starts to pour into the second bucket. Suddenly you feel hot liquid running down your leg. You take the buckets off of your shoulders and shake your pant leg.

"What's wrong, Dylan?" David asks.

The bucket has a hole in the bottom. Fang sighs and begins to check the other buckets. You look at Christopher and David. They look back at you with raised eyebrows--more sabotage.

Choose Your Own Track: Do you choose to carry tea to the men? Go to page 51.

Choose Your Own Track: Do you choose to leave now before anyone else is hurt? Go to page 59.

Chinese Tea Carrier

"We just talked to the engineer. He'll let us up in the locomotive," David says.

You walk over the locomotives. The engineer is in the cab. He looks out, "Do you boys need anything else?"

"Can we come see the locomotives?" Christopher asks.

"You can come up for a look if you promise not to touch anything," the engineer says. "Come up now before we have to move again."

The train is not moving so, all three of you climb into the small space behind the engineer's seat. Behind the cab of the locomotive, you can see the engineer tossing small logs into the firebox. The engineer has a row of dials in front of him. Over his head, you can see the handle for the whistle.

You can feel the amount of power that the locomotive has. The floor rumbles under your feet and it is hard to hear someone talking. It would be so exciting to be an engineer driving this locomotive.

The engineer points to the gauges for the amount of steam, to the throttle to slow down or speed up the engine and the brake handle.

Then he says, "You boys better get down. I can't have you up here long because it can be dangerous."

"Can we blow the whistle?" Christopher asks. You nod your head because you wanted to do it.

The engineer says, "Since you asked, young man, you can blow one short toot when it is time to move forward. Just one short one to tell everyone that we are moving forward. A longer one would mean other things, like danger or time to quit for the day.

You soak in move of the locomotive atmosphere for a few more minutes. Then the engineer says, "It's time to move forward." He puts his hand on the throttle and nods to Christopher. "You give one short blast and then you all jump down. I'll wait until you are clear before we

24

move. Good luck to you."

"Thank you, sir." You say.

Christopher reaches up to the whistle handle and gives it a short pull. The sound blasts out and you, David and Christopher jump out the door of the locomotive. The engineer waves as the train begins to inch forward.

"We better go check out the wagons," David says. "I have a feeling that I saw something important, but I can't figure out what it was."

You agree, "We should try to find a few more clues about the thief."

Choose Your Own Track: Go to page 29.

Wagons bring supplies for the construction

The snow is moving faster. All three of you are struggling to get out of the ropes and you can hear that Christopher is saying, "Hurry! Hurry!" under his breath.

But the snow is accelerating. Just as the ropes fall off of your legs, the snow hits you. It doesn't feel like fluffy snowflakes. It feels like being hit by a train. You are swallowed up by the snow. You try to push yourself up, but the snow is carrying you over the train track and toward the canyon.

So much snow is pressed into your face that you can't breathe. You throw your arms around trying to find a way out. You have no idea where the other boys are. You are dragged along the rocks at the edge of the canyon and you feel the drop as the snow carries you over the edge.

Choose Your Own Track: Go to page 36.

You decide to go to the railroad site. You hold a finger against the watch as David uses one finger to lift the first crystal. He manages to turn the crystal, but he can't see where the hand is pointing.

"Christopher, can you see the hand?" you ask.

Christopher says he can, so he tells David to turn the crystal slowly. He says stop when the hand is pointing to 3, back to the east. Then David pushes down on the crystal.

The dark and squeezing begins. It's even worse this time because Christopher and David are jammed up against your back and your side. But when you open your eyes, you are near the wagons at the back of the train.

"We need to find Mack Brown and tell him about the Indians," you say. The other boys agree, so you begin to skip and shuffle toward the locomotives. As you pass the first one, the engineer leans out and yells, "What's wrong, boys? Who tied you up?"

The fireman jumps down out of the engine and cuts through the straps around your arms. You tell the engineer, "Indians captured us, but we got away. They might come to attack the train."

"I can take care of that," the engineer says. He puts his hand up on the whistle chain and blows three quick toots of the whistle.

"That's our warning signal," the fireman tells you.

Sure enough, you start to see men crowd into the cars of the train. When they jump back down, they are carrying the rifles you saw earlier. Groups of them spread out on both sides of the track. The other men who are wagon drivers and tracklayers keep working, as the armed group guards the train.

You see Mack Brown hurrying along the track to the first engine. He stops when he sees you.

"These boys were grabbed by Indians," the fireman says. "So we sounded the alarm."

27

"Glad you are safe, boys," Mack says. "Follow me."

You thank the engineer and the fireman for their help. Then you walk along the tracks for a short length and Mack turns to speak to you. "Are you boys really all right?"

"We're fine," you tell him. "But we still don't know who the thieves are."

"Maybe you should go back to Mr. Chaney," Mack says. "We will have to deal with the thieves ourselves."

"We agreed that we are still going to find out something about the thieves," you tell him.

He looks at you a moment and then says, "Let me know if you find out anything. And be careful!"

Choose Your Track: go to page 29

You all three agree to check out the wagons, so you creep behind a small hill. Once you are out of sight of the train and the men, you pull the watch out of your pocket. When you open the crystal, you see that only one and a half hours are left before you have to get home or you will be stuck in the 1860s.

"We've got to do this fast," you tell Christopher and David.

You line the hand up to the 3 to go east and do one short push down. You are across the track from the wagons. You can see a few men around the wagons, so you creep along trying to stay out of their sight.

As you crouch next to a wagon wheel, you realize that the wind is starting to blow and it feels cool. The sky is darker with big clouds building up right over you. It looks like a thunderstorm is coming.

You turn to tell Christopher and David that you need to find some shelter when suddenly there is a flash of lightning and a few seconds later, the thunder rolls.

"Let's get in a wagon," Christopher says at the same time that David says, "Let's go back to the locomotives."

Which would be better? you wonder.

"Do we need to do rock, paper, scissors?" David asks.

All three of you make a fist and pound it into your hand.

Choose Your Track: Do you choose to hide in a wagon? Go to page45

Choose Your Track: Do you choose to run for a locomotive to hide in? Go to page 42

He glares at all three of you and then says, "Here are the rules for train travel through time. First, you must all stick together. If you are separated and have to come back here, one of you might not make it. You will be stuck in the past forever. Second, you must not tell anyone there that you are from the future and you can't tell anyone here that you traveled in time. Third, when you have to make a decision about what to do next, you all three have to agree. Figure out a way to choose if one of you wants to do something different than the other two."

Your mind is spinning as you listen to him talk about traveling back in time. As you glance at Christopher and David, you see that they are as surprised as you are.

But Christopher speaks up. "How can we travel into the past?"

Mr. Chaney smiles. "This is not just any model train set up. It has magic powers. When everything is running smoothly, I watch and enjoy the trains as they run. I make them meet up like they did when the transcontinental railroad was finished. The railroad was completed 150 years ago, in 1869."

He points to a picture on the wall. You see two trains and a crowd of people. The trains are so close that their cowcatchers are touching. "That's the ceremony that celebrated the tracks meeting up."

"A few people in that time know me and I have traveled back to help a few times." Then he grimaced and said, "But with this shoulder, I can't help this time. That will be up to you."

He looks at you and says, "You're the oldest so you will be the leader. Can you handle that?"

You nod and then blurt out, "My dad always tells us to take care of each other."

"Yeah," David said. "My parents, too. Family sticks together."

"That's important, good," Mr. Chaney says. Then he goes on. "The watch is your traveling timepiece. The top tells time like any other watch. But come closer."

All three of you huddle around him. He pushes a little slide switch on the edge of the watch and the crystal swings open. Underneath is another crystal. This one is marked with the same clock face, but there is only one hand, pointing to the 12.

"This determines what direction you travel," Mr. Chaney says. "North is at the top where 12 is, south at the bottom at 6, east is at 3 and west at 9. You will mostly use east and west because that is the way that the railroad is being built. If you want to go east, turn the crystal so the hand is pointing to 3 and push down once on the crystal. You will go east for a short distance. If you hold the crystal down, you will go further. It's the same with the other directions."

"The watch also warns you about how much time you have left." He pointed to tiny numbers on the inside crystal.

"You can stay back in time for 8 hours and the numbers will count down in this box," Mr. Chaney explained. "If you don't come back by when the time's back to zero, you will be stuck in the past."

"We can't be gone for 8 hours," Christopher says. "Mom will freak out and be looking all over for us."

Mr. Chaney smiles. "That's part of the magic. You can spend hours in the past, but only minutes will go by here while you are gone."

"How do we come back?" you ask.

"The stem of the watch handles that. You might not be familiar with this kind of watch, but this part sticking out is the stem. When the top crystal is down in place and you pull out the stem, you can make the hands of the watch move, the hands that tell time. Then you push it back in and the time is reset."

"Does it work to tell time?" Christopher asks.

"Yes," Mr. Chaney goes on. "But the stem has another function. When the top crystal is up and you can see the second crystal, you push the stem in and hold it down. It will bring you right back here. You must all be close together for it to work right, so don't do it until you are ready."

He hands the watch to you. "Keep that safe because it's your only way home," he says.

You slide the watch into a cargo pocket on your pants and button it up.

"One more thing. You will need to know more about what is going on and you need an emergency contact. When you get there, ask around for Mack Brown. He sent the telegram. He knows about my time travel in the past and he will know what the thief has been doing. He's one of the engineers. Not a train engineer, but one who plans the railroad and makes sure it is being built right. You will probably find him in the engineer's car."

"Mack Brown," you repeat.

"Are you ready?" Mr. Chaney asks.

Choose Your Track: Do you choose to go back to the past? Go to page 13.

Choose Your Track: Do you choose not to take the chance? Go to page 44.

"Push on that stem, David," you say. "Be sure to hold on to that watch."

The dark and squeezing begins. It's even worse this time because Christopher and David are jammed up against your back and your side.

Finally, the squeezing stops and you can see that you have landed in Mr. Chaney's basement. He comes shuffling down the stairs as fast as he can.

"Are you all right, boys?" he asks. "What happened?"

He pulls a pocket knife out of his pocket and cuts the straps off of your arms. As you fill your lungs with air again, you say, "The Indians grabbed us. We barely got away."

"I should have warned you about them. They are not at all happy with the railroad being built through their land," Mr. Chaney says, as you boys rub your arms where the straps were so tight. "And they are right that the railroad will completely change their lives."

Then he goes on, "Were you able to figure out who the thief is?"

You shake your head. Before you can say anything, David holds out the watch. "I think it's time for us to go back and play with our Legos," he says.

Christopher nods and says, "Enough of real trains for now."

Choose Your Own Track: Go to page 19.

When you pass the locomotives, you find a whole group of wagons. Some of them have drivers on the seat, but many are sitting along the track. As you get close to one wagon, a boy jumps out.

"Are you the boy sent to help?" he asks you.

"Sure, I guess," you say.

"My name is Conor," the boy says.

"I'm Dylan and this is Christopher and David."

"Why did you bring those little boys along?" he says.

"Hey, we're not little," Christopher protests.

"They are my brother and my cousin," you explain. "I have to keep an eye on them." You frown at Christopher, hoping he will get the message to keep quiet.

Conor points to a group of three wagons close to each other.

"We have to put these two loads together, so that this wagon can head back to Omaha to get more supplies. The man in charge wants to leave in a couple of hours, so we have to get to work."

You climb up into the wagon and Christopher and David stay on the ground. The wagon is full of sacks. Some say flour on the side and some say beans. Boxes with railroad spikes are along the sides of the wagon.

Conor says, "Leave those heavy sacks. They weigh 100 pounds, so Big Brian will get them later."

You pick up a box and hand it down to Christopher and David. Together they lug the heavy box over to the other wagon and together heave it up to Conor. By the time they are back to your wagon, you have another box ready for them. You get hotter and stickier as you work.

In a little while, a huge man sticks his face around the wagon. "What are little boys doing here?" he says with a growl and a frown. His red hair and beard bristle out from his head and face.

"They are helping me, Big Brian," Conor says. "We have almost unloaded the boxes, so give us a bit and you can get the big bags."

When the boxes are finished, Conor says he has to go to the dining car. You boys sit on the ground for a rest. You lean back against a nearby wagon.

"I wonder why this wagon has a red bandanna on it," David asks.

You see a bandanna tied to part of the wagon seat. No one has an answer to David's question. You wonder, *What should you do next to figure out who the thieves are?*

Big Brian comes around the front of the wagon and spots the three of you sitting there.

"What do you think you are doing, you brats?" he yells. "Get away from my wagon." He starts towards you with clenched fists.

The three of you quickly scurry between the other wagons and get as far away from him as possible.

"Whew, that is one mad guy," Christopher says.

"Where should we go next?" you ask.

"Dining car," Christopher says at the same time that David says, "Find something to eat."

"Maybe we can find something here," you say.

Choose Your Track: Do you choose to go to the dining car? Go to page 10.

Choose Your Track: Do you choose to look around in the wagons for something to eat? Go to page 38.

You feel yourself going over the edge of the canyon. *We're going to die,* you think. You try to flail your arms around to get loose from the snow. But it keeps pushing and tumbling you along. Someone's shoe hits you in the head and it hurts all over again from the punch from the green hat man.

Finally when your lungs are about to burst for trying to get air, you can feel that you are slowing down. Then you slide to a stop. Immediately you start to push against the snow. You have to get out so you can breathe. *But which way is up?* You keep thrashing around and suddenly, one arm pushes through the snow. You throw your body that way and your head pokes up into the air.

You push your way out of the snow while you gulp in the cold air. You look around for any sign of Christopher and David. Your heart sinks as you don't see them. Then you catch a glimpse of David's red mitten. You grab the hand inside the mitten and begin to pull. David flounders around holding on to your hand. Finally, his head pops up out of the snow and you finish digging him out. All the time, you are desperately scanning for any sign of Christopher.

After David stands up and draws in a big lungful of air, he says, "Where is Christopher?"

You are stomping through the snow, looking. Finally, with relief, you see the top pompom of Christopher's hat. You and David struggle through the snow to reach Christopher just as the hat begins to move. You quickly dig out around Christopher's head and he begins to pull in air.

The three of you have snow plastered to your body and you are all shivering. Christopher says in a shaky, shivering voice, "It's time to go home."

All of you stand close together and you pull out the watch and push on the stem.

Just as the squeezing feeling begins, the snow under your feet begins to slide, carrying you along with it. David realizes that you are moving away from them and he tries to grab you, but you are moving too fast.

You still feel the squeezing travel feeling, but all you can think of is *where am I going?*

Choose Your Own Track: Go to page 39.

You, Christopher and David start looking for a wagon that might have food that is easy to eat.

"Do you think they have snacks in this time?" you ask the other boys, as you climb up to look inside a wagon.

"What are you stealing?" a man comes up behind you.

You freeze, but David finds his voice and says, "We're not stealing. We're looking for something to eat."

"If you don't get out of here, I'll turn you into something the coyotes will eat," the man says as he grabs at Christopher's arm. Christopher spins away and all three of you run as quickly as you can. You hide under a nearby wagon. You watch as the man climbs into the wagon that you had just been on. Pretty soon, he jumps down and takes off.

"Let's go to the dining car," David says. "We gotta eat something."

Christopher says, rubbing his arm, "This is getting more dangerous. Should we go home?"

Choose Your Track: Do you choose the dining car? Go to page 10.

Choose Your Track: Do you choose to go home? Go to page 19

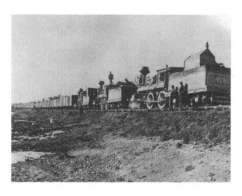

Backward Train

When the black squeezing stops, you keep your eyes closed. *What will you see when you open them?* You can feel warm air. It's warm inside your coat and you can feel snow melting and running down inside your shirt.

You take a big breath and open your eyes. You are not in Mr. Chaney's basement. You whirl around, but Christopher and David are not in sight. *Where can they be? Did they get stuck in the past?*

You take a few breaths and look around. Now you know where you are. You landed two streets over from your house and Mr. Chaney's.

You slide out of your coat and jog to the corner. You want to get back to Mr. Chaney's so you can find Christopher and David. If anything happened to them, it will be your fault.

You pound on Mr. Chaney's door and it quickly opens. Christopher and David grab you for a big group hug. "Dylan, we were afraid you got stuck back there," Christopher says.

Mr. Chaney reaches out to ruffle your hair and says, "You had us worried."

"I was worried about you," you tell the other boys.

You explain what happened to you as all of you head downstairs. Just as you reach the bottom, the telegraph dings. Mr. Chaney strides over to it and quickly decodes the message. He smiles and says, "You boys did it. That green hat man was sabotaging the railroad. He invested money in another railroad, so he wanted Central Pacific to fail. Then his company would take over. Great job!"

Then he goes on, "If you can come over tomorrow or the next day, I will have a special treat for you. You have earned it."

Christopher says, "We are going to the zoo tomorrow, but we'll be here the next day."

David chimes in, "What is the treat?"

Mr. Chaney smiles and says, "It's a surprise."

Choose Your Own Track: Go to page 66.

Then you feel the ropes loosen a little. "Way to go, David," you say. "It is working. Try a little more and I think we will be able to get out."

You can feel that David is still sawing on the ropes. Then you all jump as the train whistle begins to blow.

"Why is the whistle blowing?" David asks. "Is it that green hat man?"

"I'm not sure," you say, but something is prickling in your thoughts. "Keep working, David. We need to get out of these ropes. That man might be up to something."

The whistle keeps blowing. It is so loud that your ears start to hurt. *What is the man doing?*

You are facing that long slope of snow and suddenly the thought was prickling your mind becomes clear. You know why the man is blowing the whistle. "David, we have to get loose now," you say, urgently. "He's trying to kill us!"

Choose Your Own Track: Go to page 65.

You spin around and start to run for the locomotives, just as another clash of lightning flashes across the sky. You can feel the first drops of rain as more lightning strikes hit. The locomotives are still far away.

Suddenly you hear a loud noise and see a flash. The next thing you know, you are on the ground. You painfully turn your head, as the raindrops hit your face. Christopher and David are stretched out of the ground next to you.

You realize what has happened. A lightning strike hit close to you and it knocked all three of you out. You are still a long way from the locomotives, so you must do something to save yourselves.

You crawl over close to Christopher and David and pull the watch out of your pocket. Shielding it from the rain with your body, you open the first crystal and push in on the stem.

The squeezing starts and then it stops. You and the other boys have arrived back in Mr. Chaney's basement. You are all wet and Christopher and David are just starting to wake up. They seem to be okay.

Mr. Chaney is shocked to learn that you were almost hit by lightning. He declares that the people building the transcontinental railroad can solve their own thief problem. You have been in enough danger, so no more time travel for you.

THE END

Rock, paper, scissors shows that you all agree that you should follow the man in the green hat. When you get out of the tunnel, you can see that he is going around the locomotive of the train sitting just outside the tunnel. On one side of the train is a tall mountain covered in snow. The other side drops off into a deep canyon.

You jog to catch up with him, but he has disappeared. You try to look between the cars to see him. Suddenly, he jumps over a coupling and grabs you by the arm. He pulls you up close and stretches his arm around your chest. You can barely breathe.

Christopher and David begin to shout and poke at him to make him let you go. He seizes David around the neck and begins to drag both of you toward the snowy mountain. Christopher has a hold on the man's jacket, so all three of you are carried along.

Choose Your Own Track: Go to page 61.

You choose to not travel to the past, even to see the building of the transcontinental railroad. You can go home and play with your Legos and toy trains.

THE END

You stand up from the wagon wheel where you have been leaning. You lift the tarp over the wagon and you see a couple of big bags and some boxes are still in this wagon. You all climb under the tarp, just as the rain begins to pound down. The thunder still rumbles and then crashes close to you. You, Christopher, and David huddle together among the bags and boxes. There is nothing else you can do but hope that the storm moves away soon.

"I really don't like this," Christopher says.

"I know," you reassure him, "but it will be over soon."

You reach out your hands and the other boys grab them. You all need something to hold on to. Christopher starts to sing something under his breath. You can't tell what he is singing, but maybe it helps him feel better.

It seems like a long time, but probably wasn't, when you feel the rain slacking off. You haven't heard any thunder for a while and the sky seems lighter around the edges of the tarp over your head.

As you start to sit up, you notice something. This wagon seems different than the ones you unloaded earlier in the day. You throw the tarp off and stand up.

Now you are sure of the difference. The side of this wagon is not as tall as the one you stood in earlier when you were lifting boxes down to the boys. You jump to the ground and start to walk around the wagon.

Christopher and David stand up in the wagon and look at you with puzzled faces.

"Something is different with this wagon," you tell them. "The sides are shorter."

"What does that mean?" Christopher asks.

You notice that David is staring across the other wagons with a look of concentration.

He says, "I knew that my brain has been trying to tell me something."

He looks at you and says, "When we were at the wagons earlier, I thought only that one wagon had a red bandanna tied to it. But look, there are a bunch of them."

You climb back into the wagon to be able to see better and you see that he is right. The wagon you are standing in has a bandanna and you can see several more.

"I think I noticed it before, but I didn't know what it meant," David says.

"They're marked," Christopher says.

Thoughts are crowding into your head. *Marked wagons; wagons that seem smaller.* You begin to stomp on the wagon floor. A hollow sound comes back to you.

"I think these wagons have a false bottom," you say. "We better go find Mack Brown. I don't know who the thieves are, but I know how they are hiding what they stole."

The three of you jump to the ground. As you stand between the wagons, you pull out the watch, set it for travel a little bit to the west and push down.

Just as you reach the engineer's car where you hope to find Mack, a huge hand grabs your arm. "What do you think you're doing?" shouts a voice. "Were you poking around my wagon again?" Big Brian is dragging you away from the track. His face looks furious. As you are spun around, you see that two other men have grabbed Christopher and David.

You start to yell and Christopher and David yell, too. Men stick their heads out of the nearby cars. Suddenly, Big Brian is pushed from behind and he lets go of your arm. Big Brian whirls around, but King Kelly already has his fist ready for a hit. "What are you doin' to these fine Irish boys?" he shouts as he swings at Big Brian.

You push yourself up from the ground and kick at the man holding Christopher. He yelps and lets Christopher go. The man holding David releases him and he and the other man begin running toward the wagons.

Big Brian and King Kelly are in a fistfight now and men gather around, egging each of them on. In the back of the crowd, you see Mack Brown. Touching Christopher and David's shoulders, you point that way. All three of you work your way around to Mack.

Over the noise of the fight, you say, "We don't know who the thieves are, but we know how they are hiding the stuff they steal."

You explain about the wagon with the false bottom and the ones with red bandannas. Mack raises his eyebrows in surprise.

"We were coming to tell you when Big Brian grabbed us," Christopher says.

"Well, I think we might know who one thief is then," Mack says. "Good work, boys."

Just then, King Kelly lands a big punch on Big Brian and Brian collapses on the ground. The men cheer, as Mack pushes his way through. He points to a few men, some with the rifles still in their hands.

"Get Brian and those other two and bring them to the manager's office. They are our thieves and we're stopping this right now."

You realize that David is pulling on your sleeve. "Dylan," he says. "We have to get home. We might be out of time."

With a sinking stomach you realize that he might be right. All three of you leave the crowd and head for the nearest hill. You pull out the watch. It says 15 minutes left.

"Say goodbye to the transcontinental railroad," you say as you push down on the stem.

Choose Your Own Track: Go to page 49

You decided not to take a chance to see Mr. Chaney's collection. You let your fear rob of you of an experience you might have enjoyed. You can go home and play with your Legos and toy trains.

THE END

When the traveling squeeze feeling stopped, you see that you are back in Mr. Chaney's basement. Everything looks the same as when you left. The trains sit on the track, but Mr. Chaney is not in the basement.

Christopher starts up the stairs, but you hear voices coming from above in the house. You grab Christopher's arm and stop him.

"Maybe we better pretend like we've been down here for a while," you say. "We can't let anyone know we've been time traveling and we don't know who that is up there. It might be Mom."

Christopher nods and comes down the steps. You look around and then decide. You flip the switch on the track and the trains start circling. You nod to David and he pushes the button to make the train whistle blow. The three of you circle around the table looking at the trains and the landscape.

In a few minutes, you hear the door into the basement open and Mr. Chaney says, "It's some neighbor boys that like to play with my trains. You can come up now, boys."

When you get up the stairs, you see that Mr. Chaney's visitor is a stranger to you. Mr. Chaney says, "This lady is helping me recover from the shoulder surgery."

"I'll see you on Thursday," the woman says and then she leaves.

"Good job, boys. I was afraid you would come charging up the stairs and I was trying to figure out an explanation."

"Turning on the trains was Dylan's idea," David said.

"Great idea, Dylan. It shows you are a leader and can use your head," Mr. Chaney says.

Just then the telegraph bell dings. Mr. Chaney pulls out a slip of paper and starts deciphering it.

After a few moments, he looks up at you boys and smiles.

"Good job, boys. Mack Brown told me that you found out who the thieves are and they have been arrested."

"Can we…," you start to speak and then stop.

Mr. Chaney nods and says, "You can come back to see my trains again. Maybe tomorrow if you don't have something else going on. For now, you should probably get home. You were gone for about 8 hours, so that's a lot of working and living when it was only 30 minutes here."

trains running. You, Christopher and David wind up in a heap on the floor. You jump up and hear Mr. Chaney say, "Welcome back, boys. I was getting worried that you wouldn't make it back in time. Did you find the thief?"

"We found a few thieves," you say. "Mack Brown is arresting them now."

"Great," Mr. Chaney says. "I bet you boys are tired. Why don't you go home and relax for the rest of the day. You've lived 8 hours in just about 15 minutes."

"Can we come back again?" Christopher asks.

"If it is all right with your parents," Mr. Chaney says. "You've only been to one of places where the transcontinental railroad was being built. Maybe you can travel to the Central Pacific section. Remember that you can't tell anyone about my trains and certainly not about traveling in time."

Choose Your Own Track: If you come back the next day, go to page 53

Before you can ask the others, Christopher picks up the dipper and begins to fill one of his buckets. Once he has filled both, David helps him put the stick across his shoulders.

You find another bucket to put on your stick. Then David helps you with filling them with tea. He walks along with you as you follow Fang out to the tunnel.

You feel the darkness surround you as you walk into the tunnel. You glance back and can still see the outside, but you feel a little anxious being in a tunnel that was recently rocked by an explosion. The men ahead of you are lifting rocks blasted off the wall and putting them into wheelbarrows. Other men are wheeling the loads out of the tunnel.

Fang stops at one group of men and they take the dipper out of his buckets and get drinks of tea. You and Christopher stand still as other men come and get tea out of your buckets.

As you go further into the tunnel, you begin to hear ringing hammer sounds. Men in groups of two are working at the rock face where the tunnel is being dug. You stop to watch as two men work. One holds a metal bar stuck into the rock. The other bangs on it with a hammer. When you watch carefully, you can see that the man with bar rotates it after each hammer hit. As you watch, you see David bend over and pick up one of the rocks. He puts it in his pocket.

Fang comes up next to you. He says, "They get ready for next blast. Explosive goes in holes and then fuse and then everyone run out before blast."

You try to think how you can tell him that you will be long gone before then. But a shout echoes through the tunnel. All work stops as everyone rushes back closer to the entrance of the tunnel.

Some men are gathered around a man moaning on the ground. His foot is trapped by a load of rock that dumped out of an overturned wheelbarrow. You, Fang, Christopher and David squeeze through the crowd and you can see that the wheel of the wheelbarrow has come off.

More sabotage, you wonder.

Men scramble to get the rocks off of the man and then they lift him to carry him to the medical station. His foot is bleeding badly and looks squished.

Fang shakes his head and says, "More trouble. Someone hurt. When will it stop?"

David is pulling on your sleeve and you and Christopher step away from the crowd. David says, "See that man with the green hat over there?"

You look and see the man wearing a green stocking hat. David goes on, "He was near the pick axes earlier and he close to the tea buckets."

"Good for noticing, David," you say. "That might be suspicious, but a lot of these men were around those places."

"Yes," David says, "but I don't think he was surprised that a man got hurt. He just stood there and watched."

All three of you look at the man again and realize that he is staring at you. He is not one of the Chinese workers, but seems to be one of the bosses. He starts to wave his hands and urge the men to get back to work. The men begin loading the wheelbarrows again, but you can see that each one looks at the wheel first. The man with the green hat goes out of the tunnel entrance.

"Should we try to follow that green hat guy?" Christopher asks.

"Maybe this is a rock, paper, scissors time," David says.

Choose Your Own Track: Do you choose to follow the man in the green hat? Go to page 43.

Choose Your Own Track: Do you choose to stay with Fang and bring more tea to the workers? Go to page 60.

The three of you trudge across the street to your house. "Whew, I'm tired," David says. You agree with him. "And hungry," Christopher says.

After some lunch, the three of you go downstairs to play with your Legos. You bring along your tablet. You are curious about the transcontinental railroad and decide to do some research on your own. You find several facts about the railroad. The Union Pacific Railroad started building from Omaha, Nebraska. It was their building crews that you visited. Another company, the Central Pacific, started from Sacramento, California.

The Central Pacific laid a lot less track than the Union Pacific because they had to go through the mountains. They had to blast through rock to build several tunnels. They also used explosives to dig cuts through mountains and hills so that the trains will not have to climb so high.

You read and research for a while and then look across the room. Christopher and David are both stretched out asleep on the floor. You are yawning, too. Apparently living eight hours in the past in only a short time passing in the present catches up with you.

The next morning after breakfast, Mom has a few chores for you to do. "Oh, Mom," you say. "We wanted to go back to see Mr. Chaney's trains."

Mom smiles and says, "So he's not such a creepy person after all."

Christopher burst out, "He has really cool model trains and we got to go..."

You step in. "We got to play with them and he said we could come back."

"After you finish chores," Mom says, "and if it is all right with Mr. Chaney today."

You three boys rush through feeding the dog, making beds,

and unloading the dishwasher. Soon you are ready to visit Mr. Chaney.

When you knock on his door, it takes a while for him to open it. His face brightens up when he sees you. "Come on in, boys," he says. "Ready for more adventures?"

As soon as you get down to the basement, Christopher asks, "May we run the trains again?"

Mr. Chaney says yes and the trains start moving. You quickly go to the part of the table that shows the mountains. The trains go around a ledge on the side of one mountain. Then you see that they are going through a deep canyon. You can only see the tops of the locomotive and cars.

"That's the Bloomer Cut," Mr. Chaney says when he notices your interest. "It was a huge obstacle for the Central Pacific."

"I read that it is 63 feet deep and 800 feet long," you say. "That's a lot of dirt and rock. Where did they put it?"

Mr. Chaney smiles and says, "So you've been researching the transcontinental railroad. It was a lot of dirt and it took a lot of explosives to blast through. They would blast a section and then haul away the dirt and rock with wheelbarrows."

"Whew, that's a lot of work," Christopher says. He and David have come over to look at Bloomer Cut.

"Did they use dynamite?" David asks.

"No, at the time they only had black powder," Mr. Chaney says. "It was like the powder that people put into guns in the Wild West. Lots of people were hurt. One man, the boss of the crew, lost an eye when rock splinters hit him in the face."

"Lost an eye?" you ask. That sounds terrible to you.

"And then kept on bossing with a patch over his eye," Mr. Chaney explains. "It took the crews almost a year to finish the Bloomer Cut, so that slowed them down a lot. Is there any place else that you would like to see on my model?"

"I'd like to see Cape Horn and the Summit Tunnel," you say.

"Cape Horn is right after the Bloomer Cut." He points to a place where the model trains are creeping along a ledge high above a river.

"They couldn't make a cut or a tunnel here, so they had to blast out enough rock to make this narrow path for the tracks. Many workers fell down into the American River and died."

"Wow," David says.

"Work got even harder for the Summit Tunnel," Mr. Chaney goes on. "By then, most of the workers on the Central Pacific part of the railroad were Chinese."

"Chinese?" you ask.

"Yes," Mr. Chaney says. "At first, the Central Pacific only wanted to hire white men to work on the railroad. But then they couldn't find enough workers, so they decided to try Chinese men."

"Why would it matter what they are?" asked Christopher.

"You are looking from our time," Mr. Chaney said. "In the 1860s, the Chinese were looked down on. There were a lot of them in California, but very few spoke English. At first, no one thought they would be strong enough to do the railroad work. The Chinese proved them wrong."

"What happened?" you ask.

"They showed that they could handle any task for building the railroad. They worked hard."

"How did they build that long tunnel?" David asks.

"They also used black powder for that," Mr. Chaney says. "They started holes from both sides of the mountain and even one down in the middle and blasted away at that rock. It took…"

Before he can say more, the telegraph ding dong sounds. Mr. Chaney pulls the strip out of the machine and begins to decode the message. He frowns as he is writing it down.

"Is there a problem on the railroad?" you ask.

Mr. Chaney shakes his head and says, "Yes, this came from one of my Chinese friends and there is a problem. It's too much for you boys to handle. I am sending a message back that they have to take care of it there."

"We can do it," Christopher asks. "We found out who the thieves were."

"Yes, you did," Mr. Chaney says. "But this problem is in the Central Pacific section, near the Summit Tunnel. I don't want you boys exposed to any blasting. Too dangerous. And there are avalanches."

"But what will happen if we don't help?" you ask.

"They will have to bring someone from California to find who is sabotaging the track building," Mr. Chaney says.

"What is sabotage?" David asks.

"It means to destroy things to slow down the work or keep it from getting finished," Mr. Chaney says. "Someone is breaking or hiding equipment, making people have accidents…too dangerous for you boys."

Choose Your Own Track: Go to page 57.

"We could pretend to just be sons of the workers and still keep our eyes open," you say.

Before Mr. Chaney can answer, the telegraph dings again.

"They are really desperate for some outside people," he says. "I will try to get in touch with someone else, but you boys can go for a short time."

You look at Christopher and David. *Do you really want to risk them being hurt or worse? But what if the railroad doesn't get built because of the sabotage?*

"What do you think?" you ask them. "Should we do rock, paper, scissors?"

"No need," Christopher says. "I'm going."

"Me, too," David adds.

"Is that your decision method?" Mr. Chaney asks. He seems to be about to smile.

"It's worked, so far," you say.

"That's good, but there is something else," Mr. Chaney says. "It is winter right now where the Central Pacific is building the tunnel. You will need coats, hats, mittens. How can you get those from your house?"

Without thinking you say, "I'll take care of that. I'll tell Mom that we want to take a walk with our backpacks to get ready for summer camping and hiking. I'll get our coats and stuff and put them in our backpacks and be back here."

"Good idea," Mr. Chaney says.

You run across the street and come back in just a few minutes, backpacks full of coats and hats. Each boy takes a backpack and you pull on your coats and hats.

Mr. Chaney asks one more time, "Are you sure you boys want

to do this?"

"We're ready," you say. "Where are you sending us?"

"You will go to just outside the Summit Tunnel. I have a contact in that section of the railroad. He sent the telegrams. His name is Dan Carson. He is a foreman for one of the crews. Find him if you need help.

"We'll remember—Dan Carson," you say.

"One thing to know—the watch doesn't work so well for travel in this area. It's hard to know what direction to go," Mr. Chaney explains as he hands you the watch. "You will have to walk where you need to go. If you need to travel very far, it's better to come back here and I can send you to the right location. Remember the rules—stick together, don't tell anyone you are from the future, and all of you make decisions together."

Mr. Chaney hands you the magic watch and then reaches for the model locomotive that has Jupiter on the side. He twists the smokestack and you feel the squeezing as you travel back in time.

Choose Your Own Track: Go to page 20.

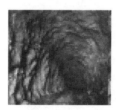

Summit Tunnel (Library of Congress)

You tell Fang that you have to leave. Then you make your way out of the snow tunnels and find an empty spot. You stand together and push the stem of the watch. All three of you end up back in Mr. Chaney's basement.

"It was too dangerous," you tell Mr. Chaney.

THE END

Rock, paper, scissors comes out that you stay with Fang and deliver more tea. So you pick up your stick with the buckets and follow Fang back into the tunnel. Once your buckets are empty, you tell Fang that you want to look around at the outside of the tunnel.

Once you are outside, you try to find the man, but he has disappeared. Now you have lost your chance to find out if he is the one sabotaging the tunnel building.

You spend the rest of the day looking for him. No other acts of sabotage happen. After trudging around in the snow outside of the tunnel for a while, the men come out of the tunnel. You know that another blast must be coming soon. You must keep Christopher and David out of danger, so you push down on the stem of the watch.

You arrive back at Mr. Chaney's basement. You are sad to tell him that you were not able to find out who was causing the problems. He says people from the railroad company will have to find out for themselves so that they can keep building the railroad.

THE END

As you struggle against the man, he stumbles and David gets loose. He begins to kick the man, but the man just keeps going. Now he is dragging you through deep snow on the side of the track. Christopher and David begin to struggle through the snow. Suddenly the man hits you on the side of the head. You feel dizzy and can barely see. Before you can catch your breath and stop the awful feeling, he has a rope around your legs. Christopher and David are hitting and kicking him even harder. But he grabs Christopher and ties his legs into the rope around you. Then he pushes David down next to you and ties him up. Then he ties ropes around each of you at your chest, pinning your arms down.

David and Christopher are yelling, but just then there is a loud boom coming out of the tunnel. You know that they have just set off an explosion, so all of the men must be inside the snow tunnel tents. No one will hear you.

The green hat man begins to pull on the rope, yanking all three of you along. Snow gets pushed into your collar and you can feel the cold against your back. Your head begins to clear, but you have no idea how to get free. Christopher is face down, so he is trying hard to hold his head up. Suddenly, the man puts his foot down on Christopher's head. You squirm as much as you can, but there is no way to stop the man. He takes his foot off and drags all of you a little further.

He puts you on a flat place next to the railroad track past the end of the train cars. Above you is a long slope of snow reaching to the top of the mountain. The top of the slope hangs over a bit. Below you stretches the deep canyon. *What can he be up to?*

"This is what we do with little sneaks," the man says. Then he is gone. You wonder where he went. But then you wonder what he is up to next. How can you, Christopher and David get out of here? With the three of you tied so closely, there is no way you can reach the watch in your pocket. You will have to get the ropes loose first.

"Christopher, David," you say. "Are you all right?"

"I'm okay," David says.

Christopher doesn't answer. You twist around as much as you can in the ropes, trying to see him. Finally, you hear, "I'm okay," in a weak voice. "How can we get out of these ropes?"

Choose Your Own Track: Do you choose to try to get out of the ropes? Go to page 64.

Choose Your Own Track: Do you yell until someone comes to help? Go to page 63

All three of you begin to yell. Christopher's voice is still weak, but you and David are screaming for help as loudly as you can.

After a few minutes, Christopher's voice is stronger. But no one has come. You can tell that your voice is going. *How much longer can you yell? Will anyone ever hear you?*

Finally, you can barely speak, much less yell. But Christopher hollers out one more time, "Help us! Help!"

A man comes along the side of the locomotive. When he sees the three of you, he stops and looks and says something in Chinese. Then he pulls a knife out of his pocket and slices at the ropes.

"Thank you so much," you say as the three of you stand up.

The man gestures toward the tunnel and the tents, but you can't understand him. You try to wave him to go on back to the tents and eventually he understands and walks away.

As soon as he is far enough away, you grab the watch out of your pocket. The three of you stand close together and you pull the top crystal up. Then you push on the stem and the traveling feeling starts.

You wind up in Mr. Chaney's basement. You tell him what has happened. But then you say that you can't go back. It's too dangerous.

THE END

David says, "I can almost get my hand out. Be still a minute and let me see." You can feel the ropes tightening and then loosening as David tries to move his hand.

"There," he says. "It's out."

He stretches to reach the knots that are over Christopher's chest, but his arm is not long enough. Then he says, "Wait a minute. I picked up a sharp rock in the tunnel. Maybe it can cut the ropes loose."

You can feel the ropes dig into your chest as he bends over to the cargo pocket on his leg. You and Christopher try to be very still while David slides the rock out with his finger.

"I got it," David says.

"Great," you say. "Can you use it on the rope?"

David begins to saw the rope with the rock. You can feel the movement in the rope, but you can't see if the rock is cutting anything. After several minutes, David says, "Whew, this is hard, but the rope is getting cut. Some pieces are loose."

"Keep going, David," Christopher says. His voice sounds a little stronger.

David keeps cutting at the rope, but it doesn't loosen. After several minutes, he rests for a while. Then he starts up again.

"Is it working?" you ask.

"It's really slow, but maybe it will work," David says.

"I'm getting really cold," Christopher says.

You realize that you are freezing and you can feel that Christopher is shivering. You have to get out of these ropes soon.

Choose Your Own Track: Go to page 41.

David and Christopher stop moving, but you are squirming around trying to get your hands out of the rope.

"He's trying to cause an avalanche," you yell. "Hurry!"

All three of you begin to twist around. You can feel that the rope is looser, but is it enough to get out? Finally, you manage to scrape one of your hands out of the rope.

"Maybe I can reach my pocket with the watch," you tell the other boys. "Then we can use it to get out of here."

But before you can get your hand to your pocket, you hear a roar above the wail of the train whistle. You tear at the rope that is still around your chest. You can feel Christopher and David frantically trying to get out of the rope, too.

Then the rope begins to come off. You look up at the snow covered mountain and you can see that the snow is starting to move. A thin line of snow is creeping forward, but as you watch, it picks up steam. Suddenly, the whole slope is covered with moving snow, coming toward you like floodwaters. A huge cloud of snow is thrown up into the air. You have only seconds before it reaches you.

Choose Your Own Track: Go to page 26

Two days later, you are ringing Mr. Chaney's doorbell early. He quickly opens the door and smiles. "Are you ready for my surprise?" he asks.

"You bet," Christopher says as you all go downstairs to the basement.

"Hey," David says. "You don't have your sling anymore."

"Got out of that thing yesterday," Mr. Chaney says. He flexes his shoulder.

Mr. Chaney goes on, "You boys did such a great job solving mysteries on the transcontinental railroad that I thought you should get to see when the two tracks link up. It's May 10, 1869 and there's a big celebration."

"Oh, boy, that would be great," you say.

"We'll go to Promontory Summit, Utah for the big ceremony," Mr. Chaney says.

Mr. Chaney has the watch in his hand and he steps over to the Union Pacific locomotive. All four of you stand close together and he twists the smokestack.

When the traveling has stopped, you open your eyes. You are standing in a bunch of trees, but suddenly you hear a lot of people's voices. Then a band begins to play.

"We need to go around those trees," Mr. Chaney says. "Be sure to stay close together."

When you walk out of the trees you can see the crowd. Flags are flying, people are dressed in their best clothes that look very strange to you. Ladies are wearing big, long skirts and the men are in suits. Workmen in their rough clothes and hats are also in the crowd.

A little ways away you can see two engines facing one another. Mr. Chaney says, "That one is the Central Pacific locomotive called Jupiter and the other is the Union Pacific locomotive 109."

The band stops playing and a man begins to speak. As the speeches go on, you, the other boys and Mr. Chaney squeeze through the crowd. Soon you can see the ends of the rails from both directions. As you approach, you see a group of Chinese workers carry two rails. They drop them into place between the two ends and workers hammer in the spikes.

Mr. Chaney leans down and says, "There is a special spike made out of gold. It will be the last spike driven in."

"It's gold?!" you say.

"I'll tell you more about it later. They won't hit the gold spike very hard because it would deform it. The hammer has a wire connected to a telegraph. When the hammer hits the spike, a signal will be sent to a telegraph man and he will send the message out to the whole country."

The rails are in on both sides and the crowd quietens down. A group of men in fancy clothes step forward. They stand the gold spike up in a hole that was dug in the dirt to hold it. One of them picks up a sledgehammer. He swings at the gold spike and misses it. The crowd lets loose with a big shout of laughter, yelling, "He missed it."

That man shrugs and hands the hammer to another man. The crowd quietens and then bursts into laughter again when he misses the spike.

Christopher and David are laughing, but you wonder if they will ever get that spike in. Finally, someone taps the gold spike in. Other spikes, some silver and other metals are put in. The two locomotives creep toward one another until their cowcatchers are touching. The transcontinental railroad is finished.

People are clapping and talking, but Mr. Chaney pulls you three boys back toward the trees. He says, "We should probably head back before they get too rambunctious."

One more time the squeezing, black feeling comes. When you open your eyes, you are in Mr. Chaney's basement.

"Wow, thanks, Mr. Chaney," Christopher says.

"Yes, that was cool," David adds.

"Tell me more about that gold spike," you say.

"The gold spike was taken out of the rail and replaced with a regular spike. They had two gold spikes, plus one of silver and one with some gold and silver on it. One of the gold spikes is in a museum at Stanford University in California."

Mr. Chaney turns the model trains on and you watch them one more time. Christopher turns around to look at the other trains on the wall. He asks, "Mr. Chaney, can you travel with these other trains?"

All three of you look at Mr. Chaney as he smiles and says, "Maybe you can find out someday."

THE END

Meeting of the two tracks at Promontory Summit, Utah

Be sure to watch for more "Choose Your Own Track" mysteries to come.

If you like trains, you'll love "Top Ten Facts About Trains." Buy it at Amazon by searching for the title or typing in this link.

http://amzn.to/2nTNNyM

61080877R00045

Made in the USA
Middletown, DE
17 August 2019